First Aladdin Paperbacks edition December 2001

Aladdin Paperbacks
An imprint of Simon & Schuster
Children's Publishing Division
1230 Avenue of the Americas
New York, NY 10020

Also available in an Atheneum Books for Young Readers hardcover edition.

The illustrations were done in watercolor, colored pencils, and gouache.
Printed in Hong Kong
10 9 8 7 6 5 4 3 2 1

The Library of Congress has cataloged the hardcover edition as follows:
Priceman, Marjorie.
My nine lives / by Clio.
p.   cm.
"An Anne Schwartz book."
Summary: Purports to be the journal of a cat recounting all nine of the
lives she has lived and her remarkable effect on history, beginning in
Mesopotamia in 3000 B.C. and culminating in Wisconsin in 1995.
ISBN 0-689-81135-7 (hc.)
[1. Cats—Fiction. 2. World history—Fiction. 3. Diaries—Fiction.] I. Title.
PZ7.P932My   1998
[E]—dc21
97-47565
ISBN 0-689-84670-3 (Aladdin pbk.)

My Nine Lives

by Clio

ALADDIN PAPERBACKS
New York London Toronto Sydney Singapore

A note from the Publisher:
One recent morning, we received a large brown envelope in the mail. It contained a tattered old book and the following letter:

Dear Publisher,

I have stumbled upon a remark-able discovery. While searching the house for my cat, Clio, I found what looked like her journal under an old couch. Although Clio is awfully clever, I never knew her talents extended beyond climbing drapes and prying the lids off cheese containers—until now.

Might you be interested in publishing this?

Yours truly,

Mamie Pennyfellow

FIRST CLASS MAIL

JUNE 17
2 PM

Atheneum Books for Young Readers
1230 Avenue of the Americas
New York, New York 10020

RUSH!

At first we thought it was a hoax. But after careful examination, the book truly appears to be the journal of a cat who has lived nine different lives in nine different historical times! We decided we couldn't keep this important document a secret. So we've published the highlights for you to read.

Life # 1
Mesopotamia
3000 B.C.

me

Alive! I yawn.
I look around.
I am in Mesopotamia, the
"land between two rivers."
I see fields of wheat
and rivers full of fish.
I am getting hungry.

At a farm, a man gives me some milk.

At the river, I catch a fish and a crab catches me.

At market, I find a fat crow and some water.

The Sun is setting as I climb the temple steps.

On the roof of the temple I lay my feast of fish, crab, crow, a little dipper of milk and a big dipper of water. I look down at my dinner. I look up at the sky. I see groups of stars in the shapes of a fish, a crab, a crow, a big dipper and a little dipper. I give the constellations names! Then I eat.

Life #2 China 1500 B.C.

It is lunchtime at the Ting house, where I live with Mr. Ting

and Mrs. Ting and their daughter, Lu.

Mrs. Ting rings the lunch bell from the house that wears a hat just like the people do.

Mr. Ting and I are far away in the garden. He cannot hear the bell.

Finally, Mr. Ting gets hungry and walks to the house. "Cold Soup again!" I hear him shout.

When he comes back I am where he left me, watching butterflies and hummingbirds, in the middle of a circle of shrubs and trees.

Mr. Ting notices something. At lunchtime when the sun was high in the sky, my shadow pointed to the holly bush. But now, my shadow points to the jasmine tree.

This is true the next day. And the next day, too.

Mr. Ting picks up
his shears.
He clips the holly bush.

He clips the yewtree.
He clips the jasmine,

the willow and

the spruce.

I am a CLOCK! The first one in the world! Now Mr. Ting is never late for lunch, unless it's cloudy or I'm off chasing butterflies...

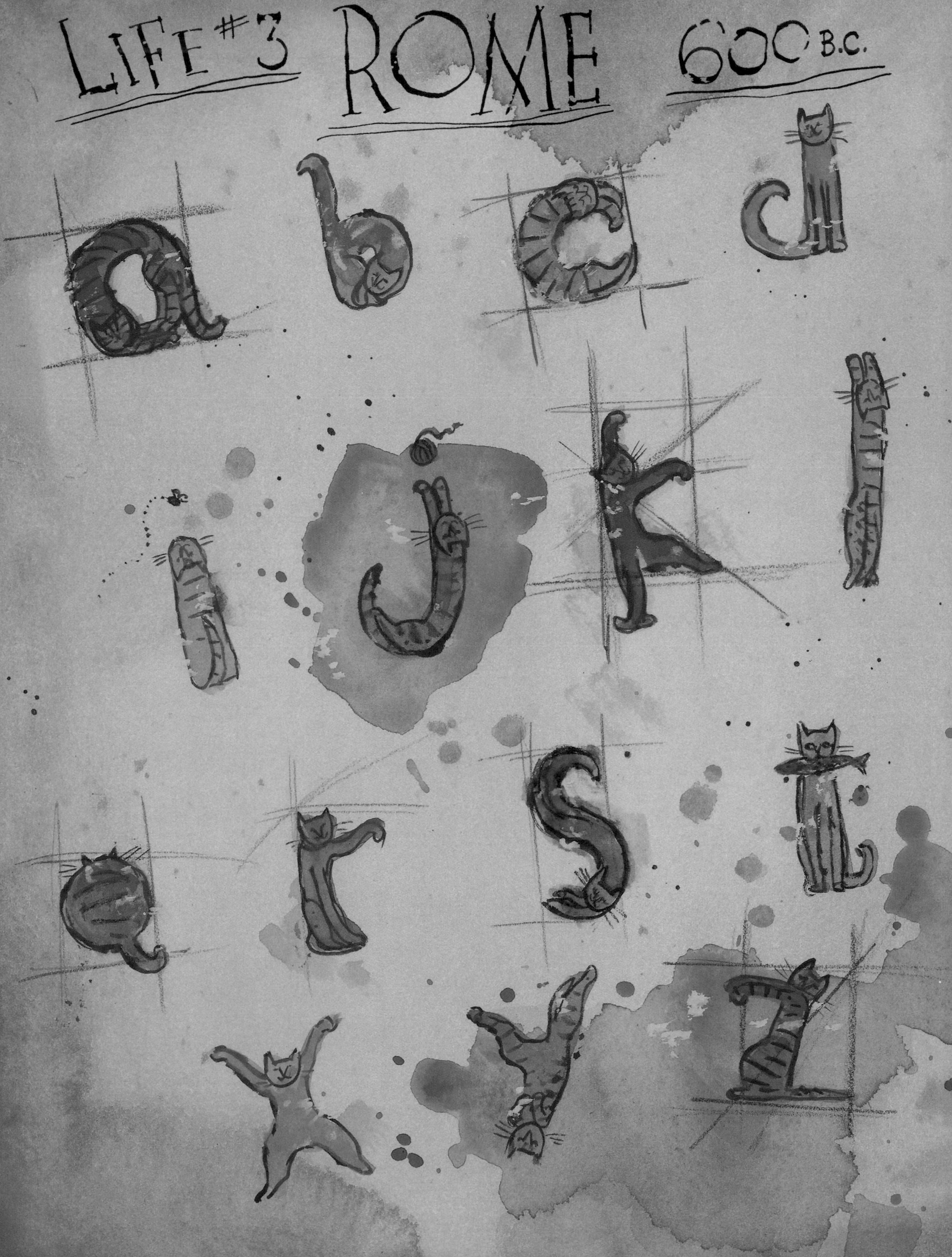
LIFE #3 ROME 600 B.C.

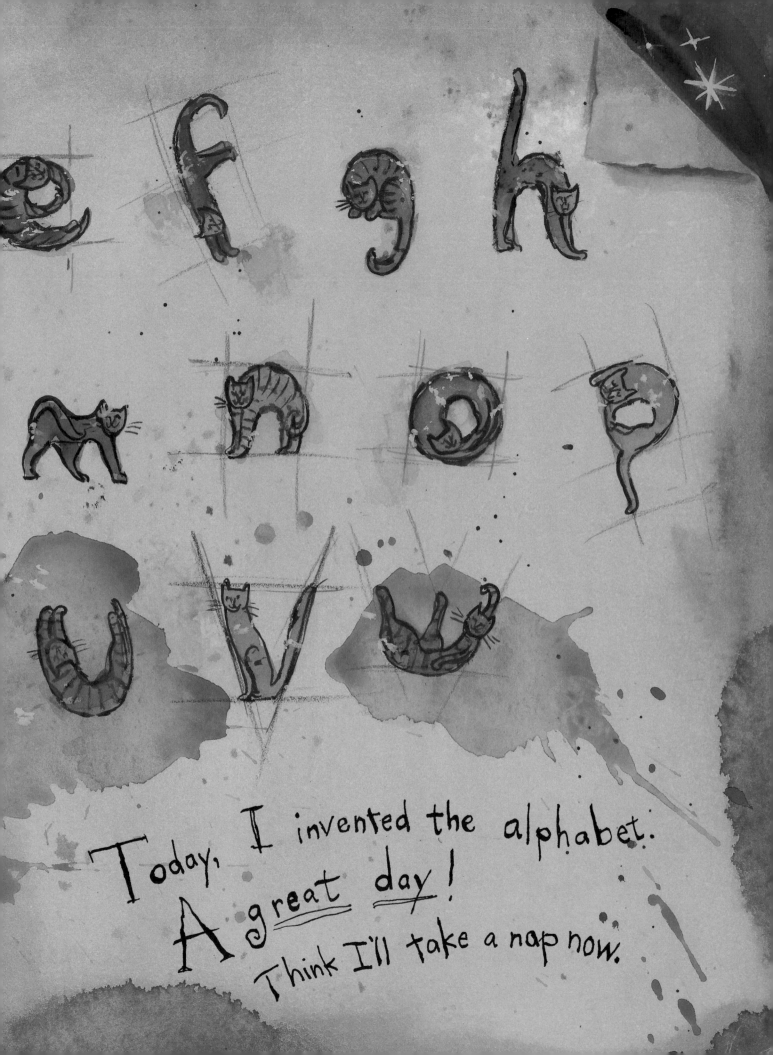

Today, I invented the alphabet. A great day! Think I'll take a nap now.

Life #4 At Sea 1000 A.D.

Today we set sail from Iceland in rough seas. I'm feeling a little seasick. I'll write more tomorrow.

GREENLAND

ICELAND

ATLANTIC OCEAN

A new day! I feel much better. I played with some rope. Almost caught a fish. Found some good places to nap.

Captain E.

We've been sailing for awhile now. I'm starting to feel at home. At night I sit in the crow's nest and look for land or other ships or icebergs or whales. With my superior 👁👁 eyes, I can see in the dark. And, with my excellent ears, I can hear a storm coming from far away. But enough about me....

Hey! Is that a bird?
Think I'll say hello.

Hello, bird.

I pounce.

I grab the mast.
It shudders and shakes.
The bird flies away.

The sail unfurls.
The ship spins.
It sails off...
   in the other direction.

LIFE#5 ENGLAND 1300

SUCH A CLEVER KITTY

Terrible times to be feline.

I live in the castle.

King Edward is feared by everyone.

The peasants who till his soil.

The servants who scrub his floors.

Even the Jester.

Even the dog.

And, especially, me.

The King is <u>not</u> fond of Cats.

Only Millie, the cook, likes me.
(I keep the kitchen
floor clean.)

Millie is stirring a stew.
A potato gets loose!
I spear it with my claws.
"Brilliant" says Millie, "I wish
I had a claw tool, too."

Millie does a scientific study.
She finds an old crown lying
around and hammers it into shape.
Millie thinks our invention
looks like a pitchfork so she
names it a "fork."

Our first fork.

Our new, improved fork!

Millie presents the fork to the king. (Maybe he'll be nicer now.)

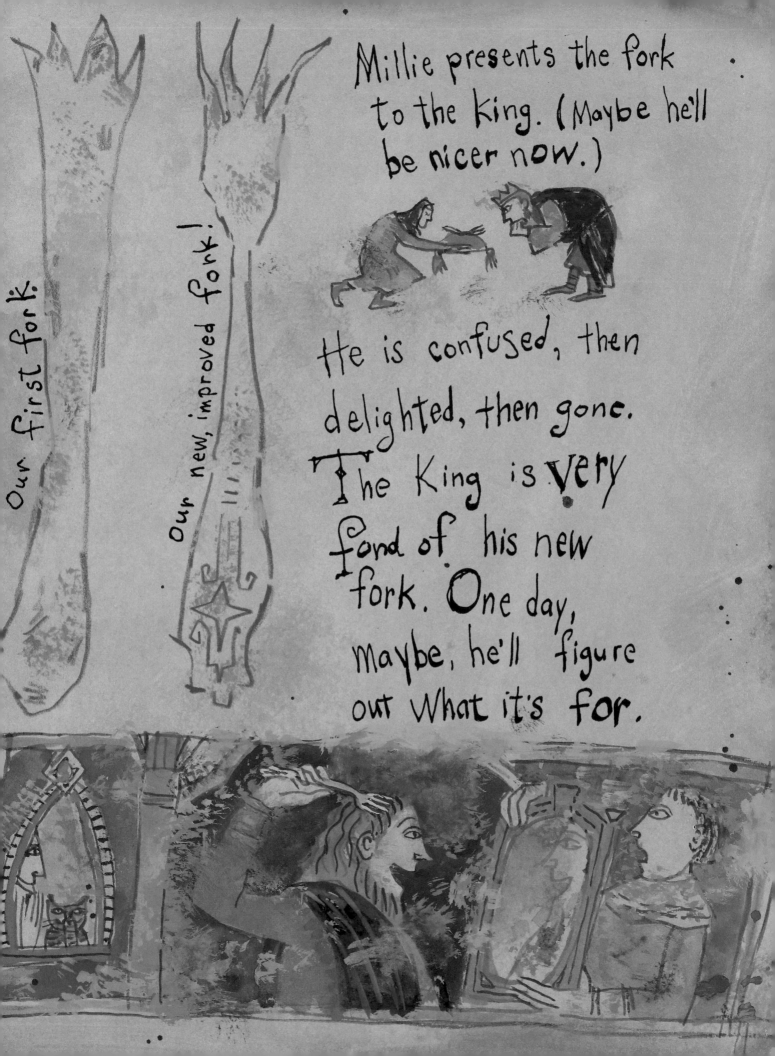

He is confused, then delighted, then gone. The King is very fond of his new fork. One day, maybe, he'll figure out what it's for.

LIFE #6 · ITALY · 1500

I live with Leonardo, an artist and inventor. I keep the studio free from mice. Leo rewards me with cheese.

I catch a lot of

I eat a lot of

ITALIA

EUROPA

(mozzarella, parmesan, ricotta, fontina, romano)

We sit at the window and watch birds in flight.
Leo gets an **idea**.
A new invention.
A flying machine!

Leo makes many sketches.

When it is finished, we travel to the hillside to test it out.

I am strapped in.
I take flight.

The machine creaks, then bends, then cracks.

The cheese has taken its toll.

Sorry, Leonardo!

The experiment is a flop.

But Oh!
The Views!

me

me again

me

Leo likes to paint me because I am good at staying still.

Today, Leo is painting the portrait of a sad lady.

I jump on her lap. I purr. She smiles!

"Bravo," says Leo. My work is done. Leo paints a masterpiece.

We set up in Paris. It is 20 degrees. Pépé has caught cold and can't go on. He asks me to take his place in the trapeze act. "I'd like to," I say, "But..." Too late. He is gone. Doesn't he know that cats don't have opposable thumbs for grasping objects like people do?

I find myself on a platform, forty feet up.

BILLET
13 JUN 10 1922

There's no turning back now.
one, two, three....I reach for
the trapeze......OOOOO oohhhh
NOOOOOOOOOOo oooo....

Life #8 New Orleans 1913

Have you heard Razz and his band? They're the hippest group around. They've got that ultimate, sky-high, shimmy, shimmy, toe-tickling sound.

But it wasn't always so. Oh no, no, no, no, no, no, no!

They were one Sorry bunch.
Had no rhythm, no beat.
just grackle, crunch,
boing and Squeak.

grunk rattle crick

shriek

twirp bur

crash bang

Then I showed up.

And the new music is called...

It's got that walla, walla, re-bop, Shoo-op, zippy, tippy, razza-fantastic-matazz. It's now. It's WOW. It's the cat's meow!

life #9

Wisconsin
U.S.A.
1995

Behind bars!
And for NO good reason!
I was simply taking a nap in a
flower garden and I wake up
in jail !!!

CITY POUND

But not for long.
Mamie Pennyfellow rescues me and brings me home to her nice yellow house.

Say "CHEESE" you're in... WISCONSIN

It's a paradise! Soft rugs, plump pillows. A fireplace!

And in the yard, a catnip patch!

When Mamie knits, she lets me play with the yarn.

Actual yarn!

Remy has come to live with us (I think Mamie got him out of jail, too). At First, we fight over the easy chair...

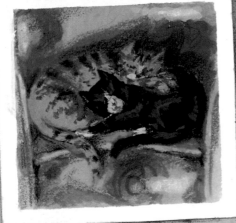

though soon we are the <u>best</u> of friends.

Remy brings me a fat swiss cheese, but, for some reason, today I crave sardines...

Clio & Remy are pleased to announce the birth of 4 daughters and 5 Sons!

Leo's first flea.

Millie's first hairball.

What luck! Nine _new_ lives.
There's so much to do.
So much to look forward to!

Mona 4 oz.

Leif 4.1 oz.

Millie 3.5 oz.

Remy, Jr. 3.8 oz.

Leo 4.7 oz.

Pépe 4.4 oz.

Romano 5 oz.

Fontina 4.3 oz.

Ricotta 3.9 oz.

We, the publishers, hope you have enjoyed Clio's journal.

But perhaps you are wondering, "Could this all be true?" We wondered ourselves. So we have consulted a team of historians, veterinarians, cartographers, chemists, and handwriting experts. Here is what we found out.

Life #1 Mesopotamia
Most historians agree that the Sumerians of Mesopotamia were the first to locate and name the constellations. Also, the pictures are similar in style to ancient artifacts found in that part of the world.

Life #2 China
There is evidence that an early form of the sundial was first developed in China around this time. (It was called a "gnomon" and was simply a stick that cast a shadow.) But obviously Arabic numerals were not used. There are also experts who believe that Egypt was the birthplace of the first time-telling device.

Life #3 Rome
Experts agree that our alphabet is a modern version of the Roman alphabet. But the original Roman alphabet was believed to have had only twenty-one letters. Our scientists have revealed that a stain (possibly tomato sauce) was concealing the letters j, u, v, y, and z for many years until it faded or was washed away, maybe after exposure to water.

Life #4 At Sea
Captain E. is probably Leif Eriksson, the Viking explorer who first set foot in North America. (The Vikings called it Vinland.) It was generally believed that trade winds blew his ship off course, but Clio's account seems plausible. Our cryptologist has discovered some runes (Viking letters) hidden in the pictures but hasn't had time to decipher them. The Viking alphabet is printed below if you'd like to try yourself.

f u th a r k h n i a s t b m l r

Life #5 England
Crude versions of the modern fork have been unearthed by archaeologists digging in Turkey. These tools are estimated to have been made from 6,000 to 3,000 B.C. But there is no further evidence of forks until 1307 when a document listing the possessions of Edward I mentions seven forks, one made of gold.

Life #6 Italy

Leonardo is clearly Leonardo da Vinci, the famed painter and inventor who lived during the time known as the Renaissance. The sketches in Clio's journal are quite similar to those in da Vinci's own sketchbooks. Chemists have determined that the various drips and smudges on the pages are indeed oil paint. Although da Vinci is believed to be a genius whose ideas were far ahead of his time, he never did make a successful flying machine. And art experts have always considered the source of Mona Lisa's smile one of the great mysteries of all time. Perhaps the mystery has been solved.

Life #7 France

The word *parachute* is French. (*Para* is from parasol and *chute* means fall.) Some scholars have produced evidence that Chinese acrobats as early as 1306 used parachute-like devices. But the modern parachute was first used successfully by a French man named André-Jacques Garnerin in 1797. In 1802 Garnerin patented his parachute. It is possible that Garnerin was in the crowd at the circus that day and saw Clio's spectacular landing.

Life #8 New Orleans, United States

Music scholars agree that New Orleans was the birthplace of jazz. Nobody can quite agree how jazz got its name, though some say in 1913 there was a Dixieland group called Razz's band, and somehow or another it was changed to "Jazz band."

Life #9 Wisconsin, United States

An expert at the post office verified that the package containing Clio's journal was indeed mailed from Wisconsin. An official at the city pound recorded the adoption of one brown tabby cat, female, age 8 months by one Mamie Pennyfellow on July 12, 1995. The catnip is of a variety that grows in the Midwest. A faint odor of cheddar cheese was noted by all.

Some additional notes:

*Most historians believe that paper (and therefore journals) did not exist until
   it was invented in Egypt in the first century.
*There is no explanation as to why the journal is written entirely in English,
   instead of languages appropriate to the particular times and places.
*Most veterinarians say that cats are not capable of writing or even holding a
   pen.
*It has been pointed out that if the alphabet wasn't invented until Life #3, then
   how were lives #1 and #2 written?
*The paper airplane in Life #6 is remarkably similar to the Super-Sonic
   Transport.
*The squashed bug on page three of Life #5 is from 1996.

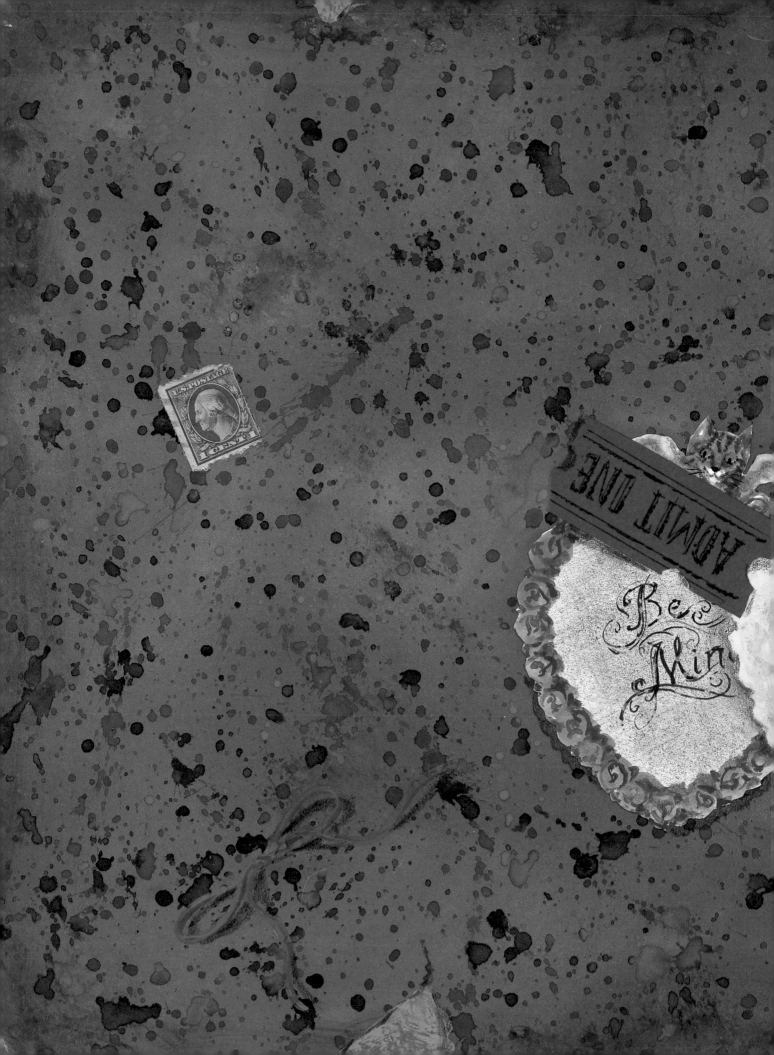

York Times

NOVEMBER 22, 1997

MEOW! CAT AND NINE KITTENS

OVER NEW

A2

ALWAYS INSIST ON REAL CHEESE